Adaugo

(A play)

Akpojotor Peter

Published in Nigeria
By
Pi Africana Press
Pi.africana.press@gmail.com
+23480 6894 4034

ISBN: 978-978-55309-5-7

You can contact the author via:
07031870062, 08077118876
Akpojotor.peter@gmail.com.

Set at 12pt Times New Roman
In Microsoft Word 2013 by:
Pi Africana Press

Cover illustration by
Ohaneme Uzochukwu
08123786587

DEDICATION

To the womenfolk, most especially those whose experiences are similar or worse. Behold, there is always light at the end of the tunnel.

Somewhere in the Eastern part of Nigeria on the continent of Africa

CHARACTERS

ADAUGO:	Young secondary school graduate
MR ORJI:	Adaugo's father; Principal of Oku Grammar School
MRS ORJI:	Adaugo's stepmother
EMEKA:	Adaugo's Secondary School Classmate & best friend
MR OKAFOR:	Emeka's father
IGWE AGU OJUKWU:	King of Oku kingdom; Prince Tochi's father
LOLO UGOMA:	Igwe Ojukwu's wife; Prince Tochi's mother
PRINCE TOCHI:	Heir to the throne of Oku kingdom
CHIEF ANYANWU:	Chief in Oku kingdom
OSITA KALU EZEKA	Mr Okafor's friends
DR WILLIAMS:	Doctor at Oku general hospital
NURSE:	Nurse at Oku general hospital
CHIDIOGO:	Mr Okafor's sister
NKECHI:	Prince Tochi's partner-in-crime
IJEOMA:	Nkechi's best friend
NGOZI:	Ijeoma's friend
PALACE ATTENDANT	
VILLAGERS/CROWD	

SCENE ONE
MR ORJI'S COMPOUND

Adaugo is seated on one of the sofas in the sitting room studying her books. Mrs Orji comes in, sees her studying and starts scolding her.

MRS ORJI Adaugo, what do you think you are doing?

ADAUGO Aunty, I am reading the books Papa bought for me.

MRS ORJI You are doing what! Are you not on holidays? Don't you know that holiday periods are for children to help their parents?

ADAUGO I have done my share of the house chores. And Papa said if I really want to become a lawyer, anytime I am done with my house chores, I should read my books.

MRS ORJI *(Takes the book from Adaugo and flings it away)* Go and wake your mother from the grave and tell her that. Come on, go and grind the pepper I bought from the market, and when you are done with it, go fetch water from the stream and fill the drum in the kitchen. Lawyer my foot!

(Adaugo begins to cry)

MRS ORJI If I close my eyes and open them and you are still here, you will see what I will do to you. Nonsense!

(Adaugo walks away crying; almost immediately, Mr Orji comes in)

MRS ORJI *(Surprised)* What happened? Did you forget something?

MR ORJI Yes, I forgot my ID card *(Walks straight to the shelf at the left corner)*

MRS ORJI *(Raises her hands towards the ceiling)* Thank God that you had not gotten to Umuahia before you discovered it.

MR ORJI It would have been terrible. Because if I miss this verification exercise today, I will have to go to Abuja next week for my verification, otherwise my name will be erased from the civil service database. *(Continues searching for the ID card)*

MRS ORJI God forbid! *(Joins him in the search)* Where could you have kept it?

MR ORJI It has always been in my purse together with the rest of my documents.

MRS ORJI *(Leaves him with the search around the shelf, goes over to the clothes hung beside the shelf and begins to search their pockets, one after the other)* When last did you see it?

MR ORJI Frankly, I can't remember. But I know it has always been in my purse.

MRS ORJI *(Finds it in the pocket of one of the clothes)* I have found it! *(Hands it over to him)*

MR ORJI Oh thank you very much! In which of the clothes did you find it?

MRS ORJI In the white long sleeve you wore three days ago.

MR ORJI Now I remember! I decided not to go out with the purse that day. I only went out with the ID card. *(Picks up his purse from where he had dropped it on the shelf)* Let me hurry back now so that I can meet up with the verification.

MRS ORJI Safe journey, my husband.

MR ORJI Thank you. *(Hurries out)*

MRS ORJI *(Walks to the shelf and begins to replace all the items Mr Orji brought out in the process of searching for the ID card)*

(Kalu enters, trailed by a crying Adaugo)

KALU Nneka, good morning.

MRS ORJI	Morning, Uncle Kalu. Adaugo, what happened?
KALU	As she was coming from the stream, she hit her foot against a stump and her water pot fell off and got broken.
MRS ORJI	Is that all?
KALU	Yes, Mrs Orji.
MRS ORJI	Adaugo, so it is because of the water pot that got broken, that you are crying as if the whole world has fallen on you! Will you dry those tears off your eyes and stop behaving like a two-year-old child. *(Turns to Kalu)* Uncle Kalu, thank you for bringing her home.
	(Kalu turns to leave, Mrs Orji stands up and sees him off, thanking him. She returns almost immediately with a whipping stick in one hand and a plate containing the pepper which Adaugo had ground in the other hand)
MRS ORJI	You think after you have broken my water pot, that useless man who cannot even control his home can save you from my wrath! *(Places the plate on the floor, grabs Adaugo and begins to flog her mercilessly)*
	Fade out.

SCENE TWO

MR OKAFOR'S COMPOUND

Emeka is sitting on a stool in the veranda mending his father's fishing net. Mr Okafor, returning from a meeting at the Igwe's palace, enters, obviously excited.

EMEKA Father, you returned so soon! Did the other men not turn up for the meeting?

MR OKAFOR They did, except a few.

EMEKA This is quite unusual of your meetings.

MR OKAFOR Yes, and that is because Nchebe, the dissenter and master of arguments, was absent due to his poor health.

EMEKA Uncle Nchebe is sick and couldn't attend a meeting? That means the sickness is really severe.

MR OKAFOR Yes, But they said he is recovering now. *(Walks into the house)*

(Emeka continues mending the nets)

MR OKAFOR *(Returns with a chewing stick in his mouth. He chews the chewing stick for some seconds, brushes his teeth with it and spits out the mashed pulp of the stick)* When you are done with mending the nets, I want you to go and call Ibe and Ifeanyi for me. They were not at the meeting.

EMEKA Okay, father.

MR OKAFOR The others will soon be here.

EMEKA What is going on, father? You just came back from a meeting at the Igwe's palace and you want to hold another one?

MR OKAFOR The situation in our village calls for it.

EMEKA What situation, Papa?

MR OKAFOR The insecurity, of course! Yesterday the headmaster's daughter, Adaugo, was raped by an unknown man, making a total of three rape cases in just two months, and several robbery cases.

EMEKA What? My friend raped? How and where did it happen?

MR OKAFOR I don't know how. But they said it happened close to the school demonstration farmland.

EMEKA *Chineke*! I passed there yesterday. I even saw Prince Tochi and Nkechi around there.

MR OKAFOR	That was why the king called for the emergency meeting this morning. And in the meeting, he saddled me with the responsibility of forming a vigilante group to help fish out those bad boys.
EMEKA	Is that the reason for the meeting?
MR OKAFOR	Yes. *(Sees Osita, Kalu and Ezeka coming)* Oh, the others are already here!
EMEKA	*(Emeka stands and greets them)* Good morning, sirs.
OSITA, KALU AND EZEKA	*(Simultaneously)* Morning, Emeka. How are you?
MR OKAFOR	You are all welcome!
KALU	The others haven't come?
MR OKAFOR	No. Emeka will quickly go and call them now. *(Turns to Emeka)* Bring chairs for us to sit down, then quickly go and call Ibe and Ifeanyi.
EMEKA	Okay, Papa! *(Exit via the inner exit and returns with some plastic chairs)*
OSITA	*(Takes the chairs from Emeka)* Let me help you, while you quickly go and call them. *(Begins to unstack and arrange the chairs in a circular formation)*
	(Emeka hurries out)

MR OKAFOR	*(Calls Emeka back)* Emeka, on your way back, stop at Chief Anyanwu's house and collect the money for the fish we supplied him two days ago.
EMEKA	Okay, father.
	(Osita finishes arranging the chairs; he, Kalu and Ezeka take their seats; while Mr Okafor leaves through the inner exit)
KALU	My brothers, I am still thinking about how the vigilante will operate.
OSITA	I don't understand what you mean by that.
	(Mr Okafor returns with a keg of palm wine in one hand and a bowl containing water and some cups in the other hand; he places the keg of palm wine and the bowl on the floor in the centre of their seating arrangement and sits down)
KALU	I mean are we going to be patrolling day and night around the village? And if yes, will the village be paying us? Because, that means, we have to leave our sources of daily bread and livelihood.
EZEKA	I think the vigilante will have to be a full-time job for us if we really want to do a good job. As for

whether the village authority will pay us, I don't know.

OKAFOR As for paying us, I don't think the village has money anywhere from which we will be paid. Therefore, I will suggest to the Igwe that every household should be asked to pay a fixed amount of money to the vigilante for their services.

OSITA My worry is not whether we would be paid or not.

KALU Then what is your worry?

OSITA Will they give us guns? Because, I heard those boys terrorising the village use guns *o*. They shouldn't expect us to carry machetes and go after people carrying guns *o*.

EZEKA I believe the King will make arrangements for guns for us.

OKAFOR I heard that the King has made arrangements with the Chief Priest to take us to the shrine of Amadioha for us to be fortified. If that happens, we can go after anybody with or without guns.

Fade out.

SCENE THREE

GENERAL HOSPITAL

Dr Williams sits on an armchair in the consulting room; Mr Orji the Principal and his daughter, Adaugo sit opposite him, waiting pensively for the result of the HIV test they carried out in the hospital, as Dr Williams studies Adaugo's hospital folder.

MR ORJI Doctor!

DR WILLIAMS Yes, Mr Orji!

MR ORJI Pardon me for my anxiety in having the test carried out. I just want to be sure that the rapist has not infected her with the HIV virus.

DR WILLIAMS Our technologists are working on all that and even more.

ADAUGO More! What else could have gone wrong with me, Doctor?

DR WILLIAMS It's not a certainty, but just a probability that you could be pregnant.

MR ORJI Pregnant!

DR WILLIAMS It doesn't always happen. But there is the probability of rape cases resulting in unwanted pregnancies.

(Dr Williams rings the doorbell; a nurse enters expectantly)

NURSE Yes, Doctor!

DR WILLIAMS I can't find some of the results of Miss Adaugo's test papers in her folder. Is there any reason for this omission?

NURSE The technologist sent her test sample for further confirmation a few days ago. He is yet to furnish her folder with the outcome.

DR WILLIAMS Do well to let him furnish it; and let me have the folder immediately.

(Dr Williams hands over the folder to the nurse who leaves with utmost urgency)

MR ORJI Should we wait for the nurse to come back?

DR WILLIAMS I believe the results will be ready by now. It is for the nurse to put them in her folder. Kindly wait for a few minutes while she does that.

MR ORJI Okay, doctor.

DR WILLIAMS Don't forget to take her to the counselling unit tomorrow.

MR. ORJI I won't.

(Nurse returns with Adaugo's folder and hands it over to Dr Williams)

DR WILLIAMS	Are all her test results in this folder now?
NURSE	Yes, Sir. *(Turns and leaves)*
DR WILLIAMS	*(Opens the folder and studies its content for few seconds)* You are very lucky; whoever it is that raped your daughter is not a carrier of the HIV virus.
MR ORJI	Why do you say so, Doctor?
DR WILLIAMS	Her test result is negative. But do well to bring her back in three months' time so that we can be absolutely sure.
MR ORJI	Is that to say she is not infected with the HIV virus?
DR WILLIAMS	You guessed correctly, but that is not to say you are totally out of the woods.
MR ORJI	I don't catch your drift Doctor!
DR WILLIAMS	The other test result we have here says that your daughter is pregnant.
ADAUGO	Doctor! Doctor! Doctor! Say it is not true! Maybe, you should send it for further confirmation.
	(Mr Orji howls and puts his hands on his Head)

ADAUGO Doctor, please say something!

DR WILLIAMS This happens to be the third time it has been duly confirmed that you are pregnant.

(Adaugo starts crying, while her father and Dr Williams console her)

DR WILLIAMS It's not your fault, Adaugo. Stop crying.

ADAUGO Why is this happening to me?

DR WILLIAMS Mr Orji, did you take her to the counselling unit yesterday?

MR ORJI Yes, I did.

DR WILLIAMS You have to take her there again with this result.

MR ORJI Okay, doctor.

(Mr Orji cuddles Adaugo as they exit the stage)

Fade out.

SCENE FOUR

OKU GRAMMER SCHOOL

A group of Class Six graduates scrambling anxiously to take a look at their West African Senior School Certificate Examination results pasted on the notice board. Nkechi ruefully pulls herself from the crowd and walks away dejectedly. Emeka sees her and tries to inquire what the matter is that is making her look so sad. He stealthily goes from behind her and covers her eyes with his hands playfully, but Nkechi shockingly wriggles herself free, fully overtaken by wrath.

NKECHI I know it is you! It can't be anyone else but you. Selfish friend! And the truth is that I don't want your friendship anymore.

EMEKA Why? What have I done?

NKECHI I don't want to keep friendship with someone that will avoid his friends during exam period and only come around them when the exams are over.

EMEKA I don't understand?

NKECHI Is it not a selfish friend that will want to pass exams alone while his friends fail? Am I even calling you friend? In the real sense, we were never friends. It is Adaugo that is your friend.

EMEKA Nkechi, stop saying that. You are my friend!

NKECHI I am not. It is Adaugo that is your friend. You two study together; do your homework together and pass exams together. I know she is your girlfriend.

EMEKA Stop saying that. Adaugo and I are friends just as you and I are friends.

NKECHI I have told you, I am not your friend.

EMEKA Nkechi, what is the matter with you today?

NKECHI You really want to know?

EMEKA Yes of course. I want to know why my friend is this angry with me.

NKECHI Just go to the notice board and take a look at the results. The principal was right in calling it a disaster, but only Adaugo and you came out successful without a scratch unlike the rest of us who got scalded beyond recognition.

EMEKA *(Throws himself onto Nkechi in joy)* Thank God I passed!

NKECHI *(Pulls herself away from Emeka)* Leave me alone and keep your joy to yourself like you have always done.

EMEKA I can see you are not in a good mood today! I'd better leave you alone so that I don't get your mood worsened. *(Turns and leaves)*

(Nkechi turns in the opposite direction to go her own way and almost collides with Prince Tochi)

PRINCE TOCHI What is making you this angry?

NKECHI *(No response)*

PRINCE TOCHI Don't tell me that it is because of the WAEC result, because we already knew we were going to fail. That was the reason we did what we did to Adaugo for not allowing us copy from her during the exams.

NKECHI *(Smiles)* Now, let us see who will be more ashamed to walk around in the village. Mine is that I failed an exam, and only few people know about it. Hers is that she was raped and the whole village will soon know about it.

PRINCE TOCHI I thought Adaugo was an intelligent girl. But now I know she is not. She is only intelligent when it has to do with book issues.

NKECHI Why do you say that?

PRINCE TOCHI If I was her, I would have kept my being raped a secret, so that I can still walk around in the village, without people mocking me with it.

NKECHI The story is spreading like wild fire, personally being disseminated by the women-folk of St. Mark's Anglican Church.

PRINCE TOCHI It's sweet to your hearing! Is it not?

NKECHI In fact, it is more than sweet! Revenge is exceptionally sweet especially when it is executed against those who try to humiliate you.

PRINCE TOCHI Looking closely at revenge and forgiveness in your heart, which one of them would you say is more juicy and more palatable for execution?

NKECHI Revenge, of course!

PRINCE TOCHI Why?

NKECHI Because, it will make the person who has done you wrong in the first place not to try it again. Tit for tat! Is it not? Nice payment to her for refusing to allow us copy her work, which resulted in our failing the exam.

PRINCE TOCHI How is she doing?

NKECHI Not a moment passes now without her sulking over the misfortune of being raped.

PRINCE TOCHI I am feeling pity for her; I am regretting what I did to her.

NKECHI If you like, feel pity for her. That is your concern. My only advice to you is that you keep your feeling of pity to yourself and be very careful so that you are not caught.

PRINCE TOCHI Do you perceive any threat?

NKECHI She is the only daughter of the principal. As a result, they are not taking it lightly at all. The police have been informed for proper investigation and arrest of the rapist. I also heard that it was because of her case that your father has approved the formation of a vigilante group in the village.

PRINCE TOCHI Don't worry. They can never suspect that the son of the king was responsible for Adaugo's rape. So, their investigations will never be channelled to my direction.

NKECHI Bad Prince of a Good King!

Fade out.

SCENE FIVE

MR OKAFOR'S COMPOUND

Mr Okafor is seated on his favourite water cane chair with a long chewing stick in his mouth. He chews the chewing stick for some seconds, brushes his teeth with it, spits out the mashed pulp of the stick and places the chewing stick in the grove between the upper part of his right ear and the lateral part of his head.

MR OKAFOR *(Picks up one of the traps and examines it)* I don't know why Emeka can't handle things carefully. Just yesterday that I asked him to go and harvest the day's catch, see how damaged the traps look. *(Begins to mend the trap)*

(A car drives in. It is Chidiogo's car. She comes out of the car and goes to greet Mr Okafor, her elder brother)

CHIDIOGO Good afternoon, my one and only brother!

MR OKAFOR Afternoon, Chidiogo. How are you?

CHIDIOGO Brother, I am fine. God is faithful. He is doing what He knows how to do best in my life.

MR OKAFOR Good to hear that! *(He calls one of Emeka's siblings to bring a chair for Chidiogo to sit)* Who is there? Bring one of the chairs from the parlour for your Aunty to sit.

CHIDIOGO Don't worry, I can sit on this one *(Points to the bamboo chair beside Mr Okafor)*

MR OKAFOR No! That will cause you pain in your bum. Let him bring a chair that has foam on it.

CHIDIOGO Is it not the same bamboo chair I sat on all through my life in this village?

MR OKAFOR That was a long time ago, about ten years if I am not mistaken.

CHIDIOGO Brother, don't worry! If for no other reason, let me, at least, remind myself of past village life.

MR OKAFOR Okay, if that is your choice.

CHIDIOGO *(Sees Emeka's brother bringing the chair)* Don't worry. Take it back.

MR OKAFOR This is a new habit you are learning *o*. You no longer inform anybody that you are coming. You will just appear unannounced.

CHIDIOGO When I left Lagos in the morning, I didn't plan to come to the village. My plan was to just attend the burial ceremony of my friend's mother at Owerri. It was after the burial that I changed my mind.

MR OKAFOR So you would have come to Owerri and returned to Lagos without coming to say hi to us in the village?

CHIDIOGO That was what I thought of and decided to come.

MR OKAFOR If you had informed me that you were coming, I would have reserved some fresh fish for you to take back to Lagos. It is less than an hour ago that Emeka took them to supply to Chief Anyanwu.

CHIDIOGO Brother, don't worry. Next time I will go with fresh fish. How is Emeka? I guess he hasn't returned from the fish supplies.

MR OKAFOR He said he would also go to check his WAEC result.

CHIDIOGO Oh! I remember he actually told me, the last time I came, that he was preparing for that exam.

MR OKAFOR He sat for the exams about two months ago.

CHIDIOGO That is great. Now, I hope you will allow him come with me to Lagos, because his schooling has always been your excuse for not allowing him come with me to Lagos.

MR OKAFOR Not that I don't want him to go with you to Lagos, but the expenses will be too much for you. Chioma and Chinedu are yet to complete their university education and you are the one sponsoring them.

CHIDIOGO And who says adding Emeka is too big a sacrifice for me to make!

MR OKAFOR I think it is too big.

CHIDIOGO Brother, no sacrifice can equate with what you have done for me. After the death of Papa, you sacrificed your education to make me who I am today.

MR OKAFOR You are my younger sister. So it was my responsibility to take care of you after the death of our father. That was only what I did and nothing more. Anyway, if you know Emeka's education won't be too much of a burden for you, you can go with him.

CHIDIOGO It won't!

(Emeka returns. He sees Chidiogo's car in the middle of the compound and

Chidiogo chatting with his father. Goes straight to greet her)

EMEKA Good afternoon, Aunty. When did you arrive?

CHIDIOGO Afternoon, Emeka! I arrived about thirty minutes ago. See how you are growing taller and taller every day. Very soon you will be taller than your father.

(Emeka smiles; turns to his father and gives him the good news about his result)

EMEKA Papa, I passed!

CHIDIOGO With what grade?

EMEKA I had three A's and six C's! I came second best out of the sixty-two candidates that sat for the exams.

CHIDIOGO Who is the overall best?

EMEKA Adaugo, the principal's daughter.

CHIDIOGO You allowed a girl to beat you?

MR OKAFOR What does intelligence have to do with gender?

CHIDIOGO Don't mind me, I was only joking. You did very well. Congratulations!

Fade out.

SCENE SIX

HRM, IGWE AGU OJUKWU'S ROYAL COMPOUND

Prince Tochi and Nkechi are engaged in an informal chatting under a tree along the footpath.

PRINCE TOCHI My father often says that birds of a feather flock together. And it is true. We are perfect examples of that saying.

NKECHI How?

PRINCE TOCHI Both of us have the same feather and we flock together. On the other hand, Adaugo and Emeka have the same feather and are flocking together.

NKECHI God forbid! I don't have feathers and I am not a witch, so there is no way I can be flying with you.

(Prince Tochi laughs sarcastically)

NKECHI Why are you laughing like that?

PRINCE TOCHI So you mean you have never heard the adage 'birds of a feather flock together'?

NKECHI No, I haven't. Is that why you are laughing at me?

PRINCE TOCHI I am not laughing at your ignorance of the adage. Your interpretation of it is just very funny. Let me explain the adage to you. It means 'people of the same thinking and attitude always move together'.

NKECHI Mr Teacher! Yet you could not pass common WAEC.

PRINCE TOCHI Who told you I couldn't pass it? If I had wanted to, I would have passed it. I deliberately failed that exam.

NKECHI Why?

PRINCE TOCHI I deliberately failed the exam because I want to be flocking with you.

NKECHI Meaning?

PRINCE TOCHI I know you would fail the exam, so I had to fail so that you and I can be flocking together as birds of a feather.

NKECHI Please keep that lie for your little sister that is in nursery school. You that did all you could in order to pass, but did not succeed. Or, you think I am not aware of all what you did?

PRINCE TOCHI What did I do?

NKECHI	Did you not pay Uncle John twenty thousand Naira for him to smuggle answer sheets out from the exam hall and write for you? But your plans failed because the invigilator that came was a born-again Christian and did not allow any examination malpractice. You are here telling me you would have passed if you had wanted to.
PRINCE TOCHI	So you knew all this? Please don't tell anyone.
NKECHI	Almost everybody in our class knew about it.
PRINCE TOCHI	In fact, if everyone in the village wants to know, let them know. Besides, it's not their money.
	(Ijeoma, on her way home, sees her friend and Prince Tochi chatting; goes over to say hello)
IJEOMA	Good evening, Prince Tochi. (*Hugs Nkechi)*
PRINCE TOCHI	Evening, Ijeoma. How are you?
IJEOMA	I am fine.
NKECHI	Ije, where are you coming from and where are you going?

IJEOMA I am returning from an errand my mother sent me. *(Turns to Prince Tochi)* I thought you have left the village for the city too.

PRINCE TOCHI *(Looks at Nkechi with surprise and then turns to Ijeoma)* I don't understand. Why would I leave the village for city?

IJEOMA Since all the young boys in the village are leaving for various cities, I thought you had done same.

PRINCE TOCHI I still don't understand what you mean. *(To Nkechi)* Do you understand what your friend is saying?

NKECHI I don't understand either. *(To Ijeoma)* Who are the young boys that are leaving the village for cities?

IJEOMA Last month, it was Ejike who left for Onitsha to learn a trade. Two weeks ago, Chima left for Port Harcourt to live with his elder brother. Now Emeka has joined them. He has left the village for Lagos.

NKECHI That can't be true! I saw Emeka two days ago when I went to check my result.

PRINCE TOCHI	I saw him yesterday around the market square.
IJEOMA	He left with that aunty of his who owns a jeep.
PRINCE TOCHI	I guess she wants to help train him through the university.
IJEOMA	I will miss him so much.
NKECHI	Don't tell me that you are having a crush on him!
IJEOMA	Must one have a crush on others before she misses them?
NKECHI	*(Smiles)* Ijeoma my friend, I am suspecting you!
IJEOMA	I don't know what you are talking about *o*. Please let me hurry home and report back to my mother on the errand she sent me. *(Turns to leave)*

Fade out.

SCENE SEVEN

MR ORJI'S COMPOUND

Heavily pregnant Adaugo sits by the veranda, washing her clothing. Her stepmother comes bearing some more clothes, walks to Adaugo and dumps them on her.

MRS ORJI Don't you know you are supposed to ask for your father's dirty clothes and wash them?

(Adaugo stares at her stepmother in surprise)

MRS ORJI Am I talking to a deaf-mute?

ADAUGO Aunty, you have always been the one washing papa's clothes. So I...

MRS ORJI So you what? Don't you know that it is help I have been helping you?

(Adaugo takes the clothes off her body and soaks them in one of the buckets containing soapy water)

MRS ORJI Nonsense! Don't you know that is the only thing you can do to show appreciation to your father for taking care of you and that bastard in your womb! *(Turns and walks into the kitchen)*

(Few minutes later, Mrs Orji comes out of the kitchen carrying a potful of messy

water, walks up to Adaugo and empties the pot on her)

MRS ORJI Did I not ask you to wash this pot? I guess you left it for your mother to come from the grave and wash for you, but she failed.

(Adaugo begins to cry)

ADAUGO The remnants of food in the pot were tough to remove. That was why I left the water in it to soften them.

(Mrs Orji leaves and returns to the kitchen. Adaugo cleans up herself. As she resumes her washing, she feels a sharp pain in the lower region of her abdomen, the pain of labour. She cries and screams calling for help, but her stepmother does not respond. She cries and the baby cries. His cry caught Mrs Orji's attention and she comes out from the kitchen. Seeing him in between his mother's legs wrapped in blood, Mrs Orji runs out of the compound. Few minutes later, she returns with a midwife and they attend to Adaugo and her son)

Fade out.

Three years later…

SCENE EIGHT

MR OKAFOR'S COMPOUND

Mr Okafor and his friends Kalu, Osita, and Ezeka are seated under the mango tree at the left corner of the compound drinking palm wine as they chat and enjoy their evening.

MR OKAFOR *(Fills his cup with palm wine from the keg on the stool in front of them and takes a sip)* This is the kind of palm wine that when you are drinking, you won't know when you consume a drum of it.

EZEKA *(Fills his cup and drinks from it until it is two-thirds empty)* Kalu, this palm wine tastes ten times sweeter than the one you supplied Ibe for his father's burial.

KALU Yes! This one is a special palm wine. I only supply this kind to the Igwe and Chief Anyanwu.

EZEKA So even in your supply of palm wine, you segregate between the rich and the poor. *(Fills his cup the second time and gulps it all down his throat)*

MR OKAFOR Does that mean you normally adulterate the one you sell to others?

KALU You know I won't do such a thing. This palm wine is tapped from the trees in Zua forest and it tastes much sweeter than the one produced by the trees in the Ogbua farming area and the ones along the Nmiri-nto river bank.

MR OKAFOR You mean those tall slender trees that look as if they are about to die are the ones producing this sweet palm wine?

KALU Yes! And that is the reason it is more expensive.

OSITA What reason!

KALU Okay let me explain. As Okafor rightly said, the trees in the Zua forest are very tall and slim, thereby making it riskier to climb than the ones at the Ogbua farming area and along the Nmiri-nto river bank. Secondly, they produce smaller quantities of palm wine per tree, compared to the Ogbua and the Nmiri-nto trees.

OSITA In that case, your reason is justified. *(Fills his cup to the brim and some palm wine spills over)*

EZEKA Osita, for goodness' sake, you are wasting this expensive palm wine!

OSITA *(Stands up and positions himself like a soldier on the parade ground with his chest pushed forward)* I am sorry, sir.

(They all burst into laughter)

KALU Osita, if you stand at attention like this on the military parade ground, not only that you will be dismissed, your lineage will also be banned from ever enlisting in the military.

(Okafor and Ezeka burst into more laughter)

MR OKAFOR My friends, three of you are the best friends I have in this village. So I think it will be unwise if I have any issue and not share it with you.

EZEKA Truly it will be unwise for anyone of us to have an issue and not share with the others.

MR OKAFOR Our fathers say 'if a man plans and takes decision by himself, he may end up sleeping with his mother'. *(Pauses for a few seconds)* I don't want to commit such an abomination.

EZEKA God forbid! You will never commit an abomination!

MR OKAFOR My sister, Chidiogo, is asking for a portion of land in our father's compound to build a house.

OSITA Abomination! A woman, a female child builds in her father's compound!

KALU What is the abomination in that?

EZEKA Kalu, don't you know that it is an abomination for a female child to build a house in her father's compound? Have you seen or heard of it in this village before?

KALU That I haven't seen or heard of it before doesn't make it an abomination. Maybe no female child from this village has been wealthy enough to do that.

OSITA You see, that is where you are ignorant! If it is being wealthy enough, Chioke, Chief Anyanwu's sister, the wife of Senator Bola, can simultaneously build five houses in this village if you don't know. But our tradition forbids it, that's why she has none.

EZEKA And the reason is that, if you allow them, you will be encouraging them packing out of their husbands' homes to their fathers' compounds at every little misunderstanding between them and their husbands.

KALU That is a dummy reason. Osita, your elder sister that has left her husband's home and is now living in your father's compound, is it because she built a house there? I don't subscribe to such traditions. *(Turns to Okafor)* It is your father's compound, so do whatever you know will keep you and your sibling in peace and unity. That is my advice.

EZEKA That you don't subscribe to the tradition doesn't stop it from being a tradition in this village. Our forefathers who instituted it were not fools.

(A car drives into the compound)

OSITA Is that not Chidiogo and Emeka, your son, I am seeing in that car?

MR OKAFOR Yes, they are! Emeka says he wants to come and spend the holiday with his younger ones.

KALU See how grown Emeka is!

MR OKAFOR *(Smiles)* He will soon become a medical doctor.

(Chidiogo parks her car at the middle of the compound. She and Emeka come out of the car and go to greet Okafor and his friends)

Fade out.

SCENE NINE

ORJI'S COMPOUND

Emeka walks into Orji's compound. He walks to the main door of the bungalow in the compound and knocks on it. Adaugo opens the door from inside; sees her best friend in secondary school a few years ago.

ADAUGO Who am I seeing? Emeka!

EMEKA Yes Adaugo, it is me.

ADAUGO You have changed so much! Is it fertilizer they are feeding you with in Lagos?

EMEKA (*Smiles*) Exactly the same question my mother asked me.

ADAUGO I'm so happy to see you.

EMEKA I am happier than you are to see you.

ADAUGO When did you come back?

EMEKA I came back yesterday evening.

ADAUGO Please come in and have a seat. *(Leads Emeka into the sitting room)*

EMEKA Thank you! *(Follows Adaugo into the sitting room and sits on one of the sofas)*

ADAUGO Emeka, you didn't do well at all. At a point, I began to ask myself if we were really best of friends. You heard of what happened to me, yet you didn't come to console me. As if that was not enough, you travelled to Lagos without a word of goodbye to someone you called your best friend.

EMEKA I am very sorry! My travelling to Lagos came with the speed of light. Before I could close my eyes and open them, I was already in Lagos. And it was on the day I had planned to come and see you. I am really sorry!

ADAUGO Okay *o*. Apology accepted! So, how is Lagos?

EMEKA Lagos is fine. But everything there is done in a hurry.

ADAUGO Everything is done in a hurry! I don't understand.

EMEKA In Lagos, you do everything in a hurry. You wake up as early as 4.00am and start your morning chores, by 5:30am you hurry out of the house for school so that you can beat the traffic jam. By 3.00pm you start hurrying from school back home so that you don't get trapped in traffic jam. And it is like that every day.

ADAUGO *Tufiakwa*! What kind of hurrying life is that?

EMEKA It was hell for me at first, but I am used to it now.

ADAUGO My father once told us that in Lagos commercial buses don't stop for anyone, that when you get to your destination, you jump down while the bus is still in motion. Is that true?

EMEKA Yes *o*. The bus will slow down, but will not stop completely.

ADAUGO God forbid! I can't stay in such a place.

EMEKA *(Leans forward from his sofa towards Adaugo; looks left and right to make sure they are both alone)*What my mother told me last night, is it true?

ADAUGO How would I know if it is true when I don't know what your mother told you!

EMEKA My mother told me you now have a child. Is it true?

ADAUGO *(Smiles)* Don't tell me it was just last night you heard about my child who is now three years and four months.

EMEKA Frankly, I only knew about it last night. And since I entered your compound, I have been secretly looking around for any child within the age range of 3-4years. But I haven't seen.

ADAUGO *(Smiles)* He is in the room. He just managed to sleep now. For the past two days, we haven't slept. Kelechi has been crying uncontrollably.

EMEKA Ah Sorry! I can't wait to hear the entire gist I have missed in the past three years.

(Baby Kelechi's cries echo from the room)

ADAUGO Don't worry. I will update you on everything.

EMEKA What a child! I know he must be as intelligent as his mother.

ADAUGO A child that has cost me my education and my dream of becoming a lawyer!

EMEKA How do you mean?

ADAUGO I have quit my education, and as a result, I can no longer become a lawyer.

EMEKA Why?

ADAUGO Who would I have been leaving Kelechi with? My stepmother who ordinarily hates me much more than darkness hates light?

(Baby Kelechi's cry continues)

EMEKA Adaugo, I don't think this is just an ordinary cry *o*. I think there is something wrong with him.

ADAUGO I think so too. Just that I don't know what it is.

EMEKA Then take him to the hospital.

ADAUGO I would have taken him there, but there is no money. I am waiting for my father to receive his monthly pension. Only then can we have money to take him to the hospital.

EMEKA Then might be too late!

ADAUGO I don't have any other option.

EMEKA I have some money which I intend to share among my siblings on the day I will be returning to Lagos. Let me go home and get it, so that we can take him to the hospital.

ADAUGO Thank you very much. God will bless you. Whatever you do, you will succeed.

(Baby Kelechi's cry increases; Adaugo rushes into the room; Emeka hurries out)

Fade out.

SCENE TEN

IJEOMA'S COMPOUND

Ijeoma sits on a bench in the veranda, eating. Ngozi comes in on a gossip visit.

NGOZI Where is everybody?

IJEOMA They have all gone out for their respective preoccupations. I am the only one left to take care of the house, eating all and drinking all. Come and join me.

NGOZI My stomach is full! *(Pauses for a while)* My sister, what is this story I hear concerning Adaugo's rape case?

IJEOMA Hmmm, the police have arrested Nkem for raping Uju and that he is also the one who raped Adaugo a few years ago.

NGOZI So it is true! I thank God for her *o*. At least her child will now know his father.

IJEOMA I still can't believe that peaceful and innocent-looking Nkem can carry out such a wicked act.

NGOZI That is why the mother monkey says she can't vouch for any of her children not even the suckling baby she carries on her back except the one in her womb.

IJEOMA I doubt these days if the mother monkey can even vouch for the one in her womb.

(They both burst into laughter; the food enters into the wrong passage way and Ijeoma began to cough)

NGOZI *Ndo*! Drink some water.

IJEOMA *(Drinks some water and the coughing stops)*

NGOZI My sister, I heard a rumour, but refused to believe it. At least not until I confirm it from you her best friend.

IJEOMA What rumour is that?

NGOZI I heard that Prince Tochi has proposed to Nkechi. Is it true?

IJEOMA Yes *o*, my sister! They have even started the marriage rites. The public marriage ceremony will take place during the next new yam festival and she will become the future queen of Oku kingdom.

NGOZI Nkechi is very lucky *o*.
(Nkechi comes into the compound and walks up to Ijeoma and Ngozi)

IJEOMA Are you a spirit? Immediately we mention your name, you appeared. *(Shifts to one end of the bench)* Please sit down.

NKECHI I am in a hurry, I can't sit. I came to tell you to please come to my house tomorrow morning and help me with some things.

IJEOMA Things like what?

NKECHI Prince Tochi and his family are coming to see my family tomorrow. So there will be some cooking, cleaning and other arrangements. I need your help.

IJEOMA Okay, I will come.

NGOZI Should I come too?

NKECHI If you can come, I will be very grateful. I am hurrying to the market to get some items. *(Turns and hurries away)*

Fade out.

SCENE ELEVEN

IGWE AGU OJUKWU'S SITTING ROOM

Igwe Ojukwu sits on the sofa studying the documents in a file. Prince Tochi comes in.

PRINCE TOCHI Good morning, father.

IGWE OJUKWU Morning, son. How are you?

PRINCE TOCHI I am fine, father. Kachi says you sent for me.

IGWE OJUKWU Yes. I want you to go to the police station and meet with the DPO on my behalf. Find out from him how far they have gone with the rape suspect they arrested. I am supposed to have a meeting with him this morning. But I just received a call that there is an emergency meeting between the state governor and all traditional rulers across the state by 12 noon. *(He brings out some money from his purse and gives to Prince Tochi)* Give him this money, tell him that I said he should recharge his cell-phone with it.

PRINCE TOCHI Okay, father. What about the *Imara-ulo* visit to Nkechi's kindred? We promised to visit them today.

IGWE OJUKWU O! It skipped my mind. *(Pauses for a few seconds as he thinks about what to do)* Okay, if I am not back before the time, your uncle and others will go with you.

PRINCE TOCHI Okay, father. *(He turns to leave)*

IGWE OJUKWU Tell Paul to get the car ready, we are leaving for Umuahia in the next ten minutes. Meanwhile, go and call Mazi Maduka for me, let me inform him that if I am not back from Umuahia on time, he will lead you and other members of the family on the *Imara-ulo* visit.

PRINCE TOCHI Okay, father.

Fade out.

SCENE TWELVE

GENERAL HOSPITAL

Adaugo is sitting on one of the plastic chairs in the veranda. Emeka comes in through the pedestrian gate and walks up to Adaugo.

EMEKA	Adaugo, this one you are sitting here, who did you leave Kelechi for?
ADAUGO	He is sleeping. I walked my father who came to check on us to the gate. As I was coming back, I decided to sit here for a few minutes and receive some fresh air.
EMEKA	How is he now?
ADAUGO	He is fine. The nurse said he can be discharged now.
EMEKA	Did she tell you how much balance we are to pay?
ADAUGO	She said five thousand, eight hundred Naira.
EMEKA	Okay, let me go see if I can get some money from my mum.
ADAUGO	Emeka don't worry, you have done more than enough. My father has gone to get the money and car that will take us home.

EMEKA Okay! *(He uses his handkerchief to wipe off dust from the plastic chair beside Adaugo and sit on it)* I am still surprised at what you told me about your stepmother. I was thinking you two were having the best of relationships as mother and daughter.

ADAUGO Best of relationships, indeed! Do you know that after fourteen years of my mother's death, I still cry every night? That is because my stepmother makes me miss her. She is always insulting my late mother's memories, and always treating me like a slave in a house where I am supposed to be treated like a queen if my mother were to be alive.

EMEKA But the few times I visited your home, some years back, she looked like the best stepmother ever!

ADAUGO That is what she is good at. She is the best pretender on the surface of the earth. Once there is a visitor in the house, she would behave in such a way that the visitor would think of her as the best stepmother ever.

EMEKA	Are you serious? So you mean what I saw then, on more than two different occasions, was pretence?
ADAUGO	Most times, even my father finds it very difficult to believe me.
EMEKA	You must have been going through hell!
ADAUGO	If there is any word that can describe something worse than the experience of hell. That was what I went through. On different occasions, I have stayed several days without food. I have been stripped naked and pepper applied to my private parts on different occasions.
EMEKA	You mean you went through all that!
ADAUGO	As if the maltreatment from my stepmother was not traumatizing enough, I was raped several times in my father's house, before the one that happened near the school demonstration farmland. At a point, I became so frustrated in life and wished death for myself. I contemplated suicide.
EMEKA	JESUS! Raped in your father's house? By whom?

ADAUGO Around that period when we were waiting for our result from the West African Senior School Certificate Examination, my stepmother's younger brother came to spend the holiday in my home. He raped me several times

EMEKA Why didn't you report him?

ADAUGO At the initial stage when he started making the moves, I went and reported to my stepmother 'that Akpan is touching my bum and breast'. The slap I received there and then, I will never forget it. She slapped me and asked me to get out of her sight.

EMEKA You would have reported him to your father.

ADAUGO There is nothing I tell my father that is against my stepmother that he believes.

(Emeka becomes very emotional and his eyes are filled with tears)

ADAUGO Don't tell me you want to cry for me. I am used to all of it now. I believe this is the script I was sent into this world to act. This is the cross divinity chose for me.

(Emeka brings out a handkerchief from his pocket and dries the tears off his eyes)

(Two young men rush Prince Tochi, an accident victim, into the hospital premises. Adaugo screams out calling Dr Williams and the nurses for help, while Emeka goes to support them in carrying him to the veranda)

EMEKA *(To the men)* What happened?

MAN 1 His car ran off the road and hit a palm tree.

(Dr Williams and a Nurse rush in)

DR WILLIAMS *(To Nurse)* Get me the first-aid kit.

(Nurse rushes out and returns with the first-aid kit. Dr Williams gives Prince Tochi first aid treatment)

Fade out.

SCENE THIRTEEN

GENERAL HOSPITAL

Dr Williams is seated in his office; Igwe Ojukwu knocks and comes in; Dr Williams stands and greets him.

DR WILLIAMS Your Majesty, you are welcome, sir. Please sit down.

IGWE OJUKWU Thank you, Doc. *(He sits down)* May the gods of the land bless you for all the lives you have helped to save in this kingdom, especially that of the Prince.

DR WILLIAMS Amen!

IGWE OJUKWU The nurse says he will be discharged tomorrow.

DR WILLIAMS Yes, he will. But he will need to be visiting the hospital every three days for the bandages on the injuries to be changed.

IGWE OJUKWU Okay. Once again, my sincere gratitude to you and your team. *(He stands to leave)*

DR WILLIAMS Your Majesty, please there is something I would love to discuss with you.

IGWE OJUKWU Is it urgent?

DR WILLIAMS	If you can grant me audience now, that will be great.
IGWE OJUKWU	Okay. *(He sits back into his chair)* So what is it?
DR WILLIAMS	It is about Adaugo Orji, a young girl that was raped and got pregnant some years ago in this village. I don't know if you know her.
IGWE OJUKWU	Yes, I am very much aware of her case. In fact, the police arrested a rape suspect some days ago and they believed he is also responsible for her rape. It was because of that I asked Tochi to go to the station and find out how far they have gone with their investigations. Unfortunately, he didn't even get there but had an accident on his way.
DR WILLIAMS	Your Majesty, are you saying that the Prince was actually going to the police station with respect to finding out if the arrested suspect was also responsible for Adaugo's rape?
IGWE OJUKWU	Exactly!
DR WILLIAMS	Two day ago, she came here and made a serious allegation against Prince Tochi.
IGWE OJUKWU	And what is the allegation?

DR WILLIAMS She believes that he is the person who raped and got her pregnant.

IGWE OJUKWU *Tufiakwa*! That can't be true. *(He pauses for some seconds)* If I may ask, what did she say is her evidence and why is it now that she is coming up with it?

DR WILLIAMS Her son, the product of that rape was admitted here some days ago. So she was around when the Prince was rushed in. In fact, she was the one who called my attention by screaming. She came to my office yesterday and told me that she recognises the ring on the Prince's right index finger as the same ring the person who raped her wore.

IGWE OJUKWU And she thinks it is just one sample of that ring that the manufacturer produced!

DR WILLIAMS Exactly the same question I asked her.

IGWE OJUKWU *(Stands up to leave)* Like you said, it is an allegation. I will subject it to investigation.

DR WILLIAMS *(He stands also)* Long live your Majesty.

Fade out.

SCENE FOURTEEN

IGWE AGU OJUKWU'S PALACE

Chief Anyanwu and Mr Orji exchange pleasantries while awaiting the Igwe's arrival. HRM Igwe Agu Ojukwu comes in. Chief Anyanwu and Mr Orji stand and greet him. He receives their greetings and sits on his throne. They all sit. Igwe Ojukwu gives a signal to one of his palace attendants. He leaves and returns with a bottle of dry gin and some glass cups.

IGWE OJUKWU Orji, how is your family?

MR ORJI Igwe, my family is doing well.

IGWE OJUKWU Good to hear that. Without wasting time, let's go straight to the reason why I invited you to the palace. *(Pauses for a few seconds and turns to Chief Anyanwu)* I called you to be a third party and witness to whatever I am going to discuss with Orji.

CHIEF ANYANWU The gods are wise. Igwe, may you live forever.

IGWE OJUKWU Few days ago, I went to the hospital to say thank you to Dr Williams and his team who saved Tochi's life from the accident he had. As I was about leaving having expressed my gratitude to him, he told me that there was an issue he would like to discuss with me. I sat back with joy to listen to him but was shocked with what he brought forward. He said Adaugo came some days earlier to tell him that she believes Tochi was the person who raped her some years ago.

MR ORJI Adaugo did what! After what I told her! This girl wants to kill me before my time.

CHIEF ANYANWU *Aru*! *Tufiakwa*, Prince Tochi can never do such a thing. *(Turns to Mr Orji)* Did your daughter know the gravity of this allegation?

MR ORJI *(Kneels down)* Igwe, please forgive her and disregard whatever she told the doctor. When she told me, I scolded and told her that she could not on account of a mere ring she saw on someone's finger accuse the person of an offence committed about four years ago. Besides, she and I know that Prince Tochi can never do such a thing.

IGWE OJUKWU Orji, get off your knees. Anybody that hears it will vouch for Tochi that he can't commit such an atrocity. It was on that ground that when the doctor suggested that since the incident resulted in a child, the best way to prove that it wasn't Tochi was to do a DNA testing, I concurred with it.

CHIEF ANYANWU That is a mere waste of time. We all know that Prince Tochi cannot commit such an atrocity.

IGWE OJUKWU *(Rises from his Throne)* One thing I promise my father on his dying bed was to ensure that justice reigns irrespective of who is involved. *(Ducks his head in silence for a few seconds. Turns to Mr Orji)* Orji Okeke, I invited you here to, on behalf of the palace, render our sincere apology to you and your family for whatever pains you must have gone through due to Tochi's callous act.

MR ORJI Jesus Christ of Nazareth! My daughter's accusation was right!

CHIEF ANYANWU Igwe, are you saying the DNA test result shows otherwise?

IGWE OJUKWU *(Sits back on his throne)* Though I don't know the whereabouts of Tochi right now, but I promise you that I will fish him out from wherever he is and hand him over to the law to face the consequences of his action.

CHIEF ANYANWU Igwe, may you live forever! I know I was invited to be a witness to this meeting and not a judge. But I want to plead with you, Igwe *(Turns to Mr*

Orji) and also with you Orji to allow me make a suggestion.

IGWE OJUKWU Anyanwu, go ahead with whatever suggestion you want to make.

(Mr Orji nods in approval of Chief Anyanwu's plea)

CHIEF ANYANWU Igwe, our people say that for the sake of the testes, you do not apply as much force to kill a mosquito perching your scrotum as you would apply to one perching on the back of your hand. *(Pauses for a few seconds)* No doubt, the Prince has committed a serious crime for which he should be punished. But I don't think handing him over to the police to face the full force of the law is the best option. We will end up causing pains to the testes in the name of killing a mosquito on the scrotum.

MR ORJI Chief Anyanwu, I don't understand what you mean by that!

CHIEF ANYANWU I mean we should not in the name of justice for Adaugo take actions that will cause her more pains in the future. We should not take any action that can bring about permanent separation between

Prince Tochi and the said child. There is great possibility that the effect of such will boomerang on Adaugo in the future.

MR ORJI How?

CHIEF ANYANWU When this child grows up and finds out that despite the circumstance surrounding his birth, it was still possible for the Prince to discharge his fatherly responsibilities towards him, but the Prince was denied such opportunity in the name of ensuring justice, he will be unhappy with all of us including Adaugo, his mother.

IGWE OJUKWU Anyanwu, so what is your suggestion?

CHIEF ANYANWU I will suggest that rather than handing Tochi over to the police for punishment, we should punish him ourselves. And after he must have served whatever punishment given to him and shown proof of remorse, we should plead with Adaugo to give him a chance to make it up to her for all the pains he must have caused her.

MR ORJI Chief Anyanwu, I don't understand in what way you want my daughter to give the Prince a chance to make it up to her!

CHIEF ANYANWU By allowing him marry her. So that…

IGWE OJUKWU The gods forbid it! So you are suggesting that rather than being handed over to the police to face the full force of the law, Tochi should be given a pat on the back. *(Rises from the throne in anger)* Since none of you has anything meaningful to say on this matter, what I said is final. *(Exit)*

Fade out.

SCENE FIFTEEN

AT THE BEDROOM OF IGWE AGU OJUKWU

Igwe Ojukwu is seated on the bed. Lolo Ugoma sits on a stool in front of Igwe Ojukwu massaging his feet, while pleading on Tochi's behalf.

LOLO UGOMA My king, please temper justice with mercy, I beg of you.

IGWE OJUKWU Woman, I cannot allow Tochi to go unpunished simply because he is my son. Here you are asking me to give him a pat on the back.

LOLO UGOMA I am not saying he shouldn't be punished, neither am I saying you should give him a pat on the back.

IGWE OJUKWU *(Stands up in anger)* That is exactly what you people are asking me to do! *(Attempts to leave)*

LOLO UGOMA *(Kneels in front of Igwe Ojukwu to prevent him from leaving)* All we are saying is for Adaugo and her child's sake. Being a woman and a mother, I know that she will be more joyful to be with the father of her child and be formally married to him rather than have revenge or justice which might result in her child never being with his father in this life. My King, please, for the sake of poor Adaugo and her innocent child. This young girl must have gone through a terrible emotional trauma these past four years, therefore I think it will be wise if we bring her into the royal family and give her the treatment she deserves for being the mother of a royal child, our grandson.

IGWE OJUKWU The best I can do is to invite Adaugo and find out her opinion. If she says Tochi should be handed over to the police and be charged to court, so be it.

LOLO UGOMA *(Stands up and hugs Igwe Ojukwu)* You will live forever, my King.

Fade out.

SCENE SIXTEEN

IGWE OJUKWU'S PALACE

Lolo Ugoma knocks, opens the door and walks into Prince Tochi's room; Prince Tochi is lying on the bed.

LOLO UGOMA Tochukwu, sit up, I want to talk to you.

(Prince Tochi sits up on the bed; Lolo Ugoma pulls a stool from beside the door closer to the bed and sits on it)

LOLO UGOMA What came over you? Why did you allow the devil to take possession of you to that extent?

PRINCE TOCHI Mum, I know I have disappointed you and father. I have brought disgrace on the family's name. I felt very ashamed to be around you people and that was why I ran away from the palace for two days. I know father will never forgive me!

LOLO UGOMA It is not our forgiveness you need most for now. Rather, it is that of Adaugo. You need her forgiveness more than that of anybody else and her acceptance to marry you.

PRINCE TOCHI Acceptance to marry me! How?

LOLO UGOMA Your father intends to hand you over to the police to face the full force of the law for your action. But Chief Anyanwu advised against it, saying it won't do Adaugo or her child, the product of your action, any good. He suggested that, rather, you should be punished by the authorities of the land and after which you should be asked to marry her, so that you can have the opportunity to make up for all the pains you have caused her. And that you will also have the opportunity to carry out your fatherly responsibility on your child.

PRINCE TOCHI Mum, I know I have caused Adaugo so much pains and I really look forward to making it up to her. But I don't think marrying her is an option, because I know Adaugo can never forgive me to the extent of accepting to marry me. Besides, as a Prince I am not allowed to marry two wives.

LOLO UGOMA Nobody is asking you to marry two wives. You are not yet married to Nkechi, are you?

PRINCE TOCHI But we have gone to see her kinsmen and have done almost all the secret marriage rites.

LOLO UGOMA Seeing a girl's kinsmen doesn't mean you have married her, does it? Tochukwu, I am your mother and I want the best for you. Adaugo is one of the most intelligent and well-behaved young girls in this kingdom. And she already has a child by you. Besides, I can't afford to have you handed to the police.

PRINCE TOCHI And father agrees to this suggestion?

LOLO UGOMA Not yet. He said he will invite Adaugo to find out from her what she wants. If she agrees to marry you, so be it. But if she wants you handed to the police for the law to take its course, so be it too.

PRINCE TOCHI *(Soliloquizes)* Why did I allow the devil get me into this kind of a situation? How will I be able to face Adaugo to ask for her forgiveness let alone ask her to marry me? And how will I tell Nkechi that we will no longer get married?

Fade out.

SCENE SEVENTEEN

ORJI'S COMPOUND

Mr Orji sits on his favourite relaxation water cane chair in the veranda, reading through the pages of a newspaper. A car drives into the compound. Mr Orji adjusts his reading glasses, pulling it down from slightly below his eye balls to the peak of his nose, and stares at the car as it drives closer. The car stops a few metres away from the building, Lolo Ugoma comes out from the rear of the car and walks up to Mr Orji.

MR ORJI *(He stands)* Good morning, Lolo!

LOLO UGOMA Good morning, Orji. How is everybody here?

MR ORJI They are fine. How are the Igwe and everybody in the palace?

LOLO UGOMA Igwe is fine and so is everybody in the palace.

MR ORJI You are welcome to my home. Please come inside.

(He leads and Lolo Ugoma follows as they walk into the sitting room)

MR ORJI *(He points to the three-in-one sofa)* Lolo, please sit down while I get something to entertain you.

LOLO UGOMA Orji, please don't bother yourself. This visit doesn't call for entertainment.

MR ORJI If you say so. *(He sits down)*

LOLO UGOMA Orji, I came on behalf of the palace to render our sincere apology to your family for whatever pains you must have suffered as a result of Tochi's act. We are sincerely sorry.

MR ORJI I would have loved Adaugo to be here, because she is the one who bore the brunt of Tochi's evil act.

LOLO UGOMA Yes. Please call her.

MR ORJI She is not around. I sent her to the market.

LOLO UGOMA Don't worry, I will come and see her later in the evening.

MR ORJI Okay.

LOLO UGOMA Orji, I came to also plead with you to forgive the Prince and grant the palace an opportunity to make up for the pains you have suffered as a result of his act.

MR ORJI Lolo, I don't understand what you mean by 'give the palace an opportunity'.

LOLO UGOMA Please, I want you to consider Chief Anyanwu's suggestion and allow the Prince to marry Adaugo.

MR ORJI *Tufiakwa*! I cannot give my daughter to a rapist for a wife!

LOLO UGOMA Orji, you know Prince Tochi is not a rapist. He was just a victim of the devil's usage. He has regretted allowing himself to be used by the devil.

MR ORJI He is regretting now because he can no longer hide or deny his wicked act.

LOLO UGOMA No! He said he regretted it long ago but he doesn't know how to own up to the crime. Please give him an opportunity to show he really regrets it. Give him a chance to make it up to Adaugo and to your family.

MR ORJI Well, I am not the one to give him that opportunity. It is Adaugo's decision to make. And I am not sure she will, because when I told her of Chief Anyanwu's suggestion, she flared up in anger.

LOLO UGOMA Please, help me convince her that it is the best option. She is your daughter and she listens to you. Tell her to come and take her rightful place in the palace. That is where she belongs, having given birth to a future king of this kingdom.

MR ORJI Okay, I will. But I doubt she will accept.

LOLO UGOMA She will, if you tell her it is the best option. *(She stands)* Let me go attend to my responsibilities in the palace.

Fade out.

Two months later...

SCENE EIGHTEEN

ORJI'S COMPOUND

Mr Orji's compound is beautifully decorated with the decoration that befits the venue for the marriage ceremony of the Prince of Oku kingdom. Invited guests and well-wishers enjoy themselves with the choreographic display of the Oyoyo traditional dance group and give loud cheers as the dance group end their performance and exit. Adaugo in company of her bridal train dances in, spraying aromatic perfume on her guests as a sign of welcoming them. She dances to where her father sits and kneels before him. Mr Orji fills a glass cup with palm wine and hands it over to Adaugo.

MR ORJI Adaugo my daughter, with this palm wine, I give you my blessing to go round and bring before me the man who is the reason for our gathering here today.

(Adaugo receives the glass of wine and with it dances round ecstatically. She dances to where Prince Tochi sits, kneels before him and hands the glass of palm wine to him. The crowd gives a deafening shout and applaud. Prince Tochi empties the content of the cup down his throat into his stomach, replaces it with some money and returns it to Adaugo. He stands up and lifts Adaugo up. Adaugo leads him and they dance to where Mr Orji sits and kneel before him)

MR ORJI Adaugo my daughter, are you sure this is the man for whose sake you have made us gather here today?

ADAUGO Yes, Papa.

CROWD *(Gives ecstatic shouts accompanied by applauds and drum beats)*

MR ORJI My children, please sit down. *(Points to the seats prepared for them)*

EZEKA *(Takes the centre stage)* Nigeria *kwenu*!

CROWD *Ya*!

EZEKA *Igbo kwenu*!

CROWD *Ya*!

EZEKA *Umuahia kwenu*!

CROWD *Ya*!

EZEKA *Oku kwezuenu o*!!!

CROWD *Yaaa*!!!

EZEKA *(Turns to the direction where Igwe Ojukwu and other members of Prince Tochi's kindred are sitting)* Our in-laws-to-be, you are all welcome. Igwe, may you live forever! *(Clears his throat)* No one climbs a mountain with his hands in his pocket. Our in-laws-to-be, are you people ready to climb this mountain?

(Igwe Ojukwu waves his elephant tusk in response that they are ready, while other members of Prince Tochi's entourage chorus "we are one hundred percent ready")

CROWD *(Applauds and shouts ecstatically)*

EZEKA Then let the climbing begin. *(Unfolds the foolscap paper in his hand and calls the items outlined in it one after the other, pausing in between for each item to be provided by Prince Tochi's kindred)* Our good in-laws, you people are wonderful. *(Turns to the direction of Mr Orji and his kindred)* Please clap for our in-laws.

CROWD *(Applauds)*

EZEKA Last but not least on the list is the dowry. *(Walks to Mr Orji, inclines and places his ear close to Orji's mouth to get the amount for the dowry. Returns to his position at the centre stage)* Our good in-laws, the chief owner of the Treasure says the dowry is one hundred thousand Naira only and it is non-negotiable.

(Prince Tochi opens his purse, brings out two bundles of five hundred Naira bills

	and goes to drop them in the tray in front of Mr Orji. Returns to his seat)
CROWD	*(Gives a deafening shout accompanied by applauses and drum beats)*
MR ORJI	Nigeria *kwenu*!
CROWD	*Ya*!
MR ORJI	Igbo *kwenu*!
CROWD	*Ya*!
MR ORJI	Umuahia *kwenu*!
CROWD	*Ya*!
MR ORJI	*Oku kwezuenu o*!!!
CROWD	*Yaaa*!!!
MR ORJI	*(Turns to the direction of his kindred)* Our daughter has made her choice. What is your opinion?
MEMBERS OF ORJI'S KINDRED	He is our choice too.
CROWD	*(Cheers)*
MR ORJI	Has he done all that is required of him to be worthy of our daughter?
MEMBERS OF ORJI'S KINDRED	Hundred percent!

MR ORJI Does that mean I have your permission to bless him and our daughter with the blessings of husband and wife?

MEMBERS OF ORJI'S KINDRED You have our permission and the permission of our ancestors.

CROWD *(Gives a deafening huzzah accompanied by drum beats)*

(Prince Tochi and Adaugo leave their seats and go to kneel in front of Mr Orji)

MR ORJI *(Picks up the dowry from the tray, pulls out two bills from it and returns the rest to Prince Tochi)* With this, I want you to take good care of my daughter.

CROWD *(Gives a deafening huzzah accompanied by applauses and drum beats)*

MR ORJI *(Places his right hand on Prince Tochi's head and his left hand on Adaugo's head and proclaims blessings on them. After a short but powerful prayer of blessing which was crowned with a thunderous shout of Amen from the crowd, Prince Tochi stands up, kisses Adaugo on the forehead and lifts her up)*

CROWD *(Applauds and shouts)*

(Prince Tochi leads Adaugo in dancing as they go to greet Igwe Ojukwu, his father.

As they get to where he is sitting, Prince Tochi bows; Igwe Ojukwu touches him three times with his royal wand then he goes to sit on the chair beside Igwe Ojukwu. Adaugo steps forward and kneels before Igwe Ojukwu. Igwe Ojukwu stretches his hand posterior-laterally and the palace attendant standing behind him places a crown in it. Igwe Ojukwu sits the crown on Adaugo's head)

CROWD *(Gives ecstatic shouts)*

IGWE OJUKWU *(Rises from his throne and helps Adaugo stand on her feet)* My great people of Oku kingdom, behold your future Queen.

(Joyful shouts, applauses and drum beats fill the atmosphere)

ADAUGO *(Adaugo dances to the sound of melodious beats and songs from the cultural band as she goes round expressing her gratitude to all for honouring her with their presence)*

Fade out.

The End

www.ingramcontent.com/pod-product-compliance
Lightning Source LLC
LaVergne TN
LVHW041134150826
845673LV00007B/2317